The
BAREFOOT BOOK
～ of ～
TROPICAL
TALES

To Cherifa Germaine Felicite Mama, for the gift of Love; to Jean Kiwallo and Charles Hounsonlon, for the gift of Faith; to John L. for the gift of Laughter; to the late Richard Walker, for the gift of Stories; to President Mathieu Kerekou, for the gift of Peace — R. M.

For my mother — D. H.

Barefoot Collections
an imprint of
Barefoot Books, Inc.
37 West 17th Street
4th Floor East
New York
New York 10011

This book has been printed on 100% acid-free paper
The illustrations were prepared in inks and crayons on thick watercolor paper

Graphic design by Jennie Hoare, England
Typset in Minion regular 12.5pt
Color reproduction by Bright Arts, Singapore
Printed in Hong Kong/China by South China Printing Co. (1988) Ltd

1 3 5 7 9 8 6 4 2

U.S. Cataloging-in-Publication Data
    (Library of Congress Standards)

Mama, Raouf, 1956-
    The barefoot book of tropical tales / retold by Raouf Mama ;
illustrated by Deirdre Hyde. --1st ed.
[64] p. : col. ill. ; cm.
Summary: Beninese storyteller Mama brings together favorite myths from the tropics.
Featuring resourceful animals and memorable characters, complemented with rich,
vibrant and witty artwork.
ISBN: 1-902283-21-X
1. Tropics -- Folklore. 2. Folklore. I. Hyde, Deirdre, ill. II. Title.
398.2 --dc21   2000   AC   CIP

The
BAREFOOT BOOK
of
TROPICAL
TALES

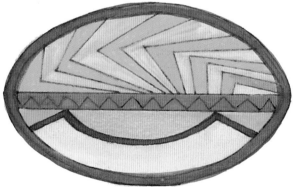

retold by
RAOUF MAMA

illustrated by
DEIRDRE HYDE

BAREFOOT BOOKS

~ Contents ~

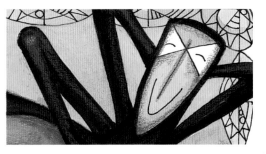

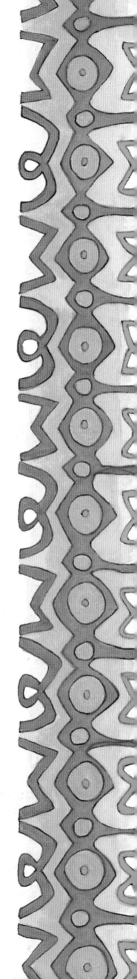

Introduction

"When the mouth stumbles, it is worse than the foot."
— African adage

When I was a child in Benin, West Africa, my favorite pastime was to sit with my brothers, sisters and other relatives after the evening meal and listen while my mother, stepmother, an uncle or a friend of the family told stories of long ago. Storytelling commanded the love and allegiance of everyone. Every night we were treated to a wide range of stories: trickster tales, pourquoi tales, cautionary tales, ghost stories and spiritual tales.

Against the backdrop of village life, these stories evoked a vast and colorful array of characters: men and women, both lowly and powerful, children and grandparents, orphans and twins, sages and fools, heroes and villains, chiefs, kings and queens, talking animals and spirits. All of the stories had a moral: they sounded a warning against the perils of hatred, envy, cruelty, greed, pride, prejudice, sloth and dishonesty, just as they pointed out the rewards of love, kindness, courage, patience, respect for the elderly and reverence for the sacred.

By the time I turned sixteen, however, storytelling evenings in Beninese households were no longer part of the rhythm and pattern of daily living. Today that time-honored tradition has passed out of existence. Much of the blame for this must be laid upon the colonial education system, which sought to make me and my countrymen look down on our native tongues, our culture and our folklore. We were told that we were primitive, and that we had no history.

The colonial education system was by no means the sole culprit, however. The advent of television, urbanization and increasing economic hardship have also played a part in the demise of the tradition of storytelling evenings in my native country. With the passing of that tradition, a valuable educational tool and an important source of entertainment have been lost.

Benin has much in common with the other countries represented in *The Barefoot Book of Tropical Tales*: the Democratic Republic of Congo (former Zaïre), Cape Verde, Haiti, Antigua, Puerto Rico, Malaysia and Sri Lanka. Like Benin, these countries have endured colonial domination and are still struggling to cope with its legacy. Like Benin, they are caught between tradition and modernity and face the challenge of preserving a rich oral tradition. And like Benin, their folk tales, their myths and their legends have remained unfamiliar to the vast majority of people beyond their borders.

This anthology puts before the reader a broad range of oral stories, most of which are original folk tales new to the printed page. Collectively, these stories come from an oral tradition which is rooted in a pre-industrial, pastoral value system very similar to that of my native country. Together, they offer insights into folk tale traditions that have yet to be brought into the mainstream of world literature.

In her introduction to *Favorite Folk Tales From Around the World*, Jane Yolen points to some of the essential virtues of folk tales: "Folk tales are powerful; they are a journey and a joining. In a tale, we meet new places, new peoples and new ideas. And they become our places, our peoples, our ideas." Julius Lester makes a similar point in his foreword to *Black Folk Tales*. "Folk tales," he suggests, "are stories that give people a way of communicating with each other about each other."

Traveling to new places, meeting new peoples and new ideas, and telling each other about each other — in this, perhaps, lies the source of the power of storytelling. Through the stories we tell each other, we can set back the frontier of darkness and ignorance. We can strike a blow against prejudice and bigotry. We can help tame the savagery within the human breast and make our world a gentler, more compassionate place. Folk tales remind us that we are bound up in a common destiny, and that the human race has only one color, which is the color of blood.

In the magic circle of the storyteller's art, we enter into the full drama of the human heart, with its joys and sorrows, its laughter and its tears, its hopes and its fears. We see and feel the noonday brightness of our astonishing capacity for love and the darkest depths of our potential for evil. It is important, therefore, that we should listen to each other's stories with our inner ears. Only then can we see into our true potential as human beings.

In collecting and retelling the stories in this anthology of tropical tales, I have gone on many a wonderful imaginary journey around the world. May all who read or hear these stories share in the joy they have brought me and the understanding I have gained. And may they be inspired to tell their own stories or the stories of the peoples they have met during their own journeys.

Raouf Mama
Connecticut

The Magic Drum

Beninese

Once upon a time, an orphan named Sagbo lived with his stepmother and a stepbrother, Senan, in a village on the banks of a sacred river.

Sagbo was a good-natured, cheerful boy, even though he was not the favored child. Every day, his stepmother made him wash the dishes, gather firewood, and run countless errands, while Senan hardly lifted a finger.

"I like being useful," Sagbo always said. But Senan always bullied him and chanted as he worked,

> *A boy dressed in rags,*
> *His hair is wild grass,*
> *Have you seen Sagbo?*
> *His arms are teeny,*
> *His legs are skinny,*
> *Just like a mosquito.*

8

Senan's tongue felt like a whip, but Sagbo would just shrug his shoulders and reply,

> *Tongues that love to bite and sting*
> *Cannot foretell what the future will bring.*
> *Sooner or later, life will be better*
> *And your unkindness will not matter.*

Then, one year it came to pass that a terrible drought struck Sagbo's village, parching its trees and its meadows, and turning its farmland to scorched earth. The village elders performed ceremony after ceremony, but not a drop of rain fell. Soon every barn was empty, and even the wild animals disappeared. The sacred river fell so low that only a few crabs and little fish were left alive.

Things got so bad, in fact, that the stepmother decided to save for Senan and herself what little food she could get. So she called Sagbo one morning and said,

If you are hungry, find your own food.
Feeding you for years has done me no good.
Shelter I can provide, a place to rest your head,
But hunger and thirst are what you must dread.

That day, Sagbo slipped out of the house and went running to the shore of the sacred river where he hoped to catch a crab to still his hunger. But Sagbo found no crab. As he was retracing his steps, however, he stumbled upon three palm nuts gleaming black in the sun. "I'll eat these until I find something better," he said. But when he tried to crack one of the nuts with a stone, it flew into the river. So did the second, and the third one followed after it!

"Something strange is going on here!" Sagbo cried. "I am going to find those palm nuts."

The river was low and muddy, but he dove in and swam right to the bottom. There he saw an extraordinary sight: a village with green grass, leafy trees and beautiful flowers. The sweet music of songbirds floated on the air. In the distance, the fish-scale roof of a mansion shimmered in the sun. Sagbo was amazed. "This is unbelievable," he said, feeling weak with hunger. "I am going to see who lives in that mansion and maybe they will share some food with me and my village."

And with these words, he made his way to the mansion, his eyes sparkling with wonder. At the gate, a plump, white-haired man inquired of Sagbo, "Where are you going, and what are you looking for?"

10

"My palm nuts fell into the river, and I am so hungry I want to get them back," he replied.

"Go in and tell the woman of the house about your palm nuts," the gate-keeper told him.

Sagbo went in and saw an old woman sitting on a stool sifting corn. Her hair was fluffy and white like cotton, and her face was wrinkled like a shrunken nut.

"Good morning, Nana," he said politely.

The old woman smiled a wide, toothless smile and said, "Good morning, child, what has brought you here?"

"My palm nuts have fallen into the river, and I want to get them back," Sagbo answered.

"I will help you find your palm nuts, but first you must pound some corn and prepare a meal for my household," she said, handing him a single grain of corn.

Sagbo stole a glance at the old woman. He knew that a meal could not be prepared from a single grain of corn, but he did not want to be rude. Carefully he put the corn into a mortar and pounded it with the pestle. Suddenly, his eyes grew very large, and his mouth fell wide open — the mortar had filled with all the flour he could possibly need! But he held his tongue.

With the flour and other ingredients the old woman gave him, Sagbo cooked some food. But no sooner was the food ready than the cooking pot spoke to him.

"I want my share," it said.

Sagbo could not believe his ears. "Were you talking to me?" he asked, his heart pounding frantically.

"I want my share of the food," the cooking pot repeated. Then, suddenly, the dishes and the bowls and the water jar demanded the same. Soon, everything in the old woman's kitchen was shouting at Sagbo for its share.

Sagbo was terrified and wanted to run away, but his skinny legs were too weak to go. He looked for a place to hide, but there was nowhere. So, with shaking hands, he served food all around, and he was relieved to find the cooking pot and his companions very friendly. Then, he took the food that was left and shared it with the old woman.

After the meal, the old woman pointed to a room, saying, "Go into that room, child. You will find two drums — a big one and a small one. Take the small one. On your return home, beat it. It will bring you happiness."

Sagbo went into the room, took the small drum, thanked the old woman, and left.

13

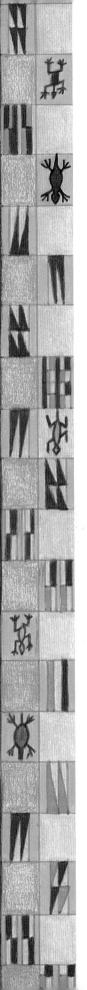

When Sagbo came back ashore and beat his drum, steaming dishes suddenly appeared in front of him: pounded yam and fish stew, red corn-paste and roast chicken. Sagbo knew the magic drum could save the village. He did not stop to eat, but went straight to the palace to show it to the king.

In no time, the king's messenger was heard summoning the villagers to a feast in the royal courtyard. And for seven days, there was great rejoicing in the village and all over the kingdom. In gratitude for his gift to the village, Sagbo was adopted by the king and numerous songs were made in praise of him. And the story of the adventurous boy, the three palm nuts, and the village at the bottom of the sacred river became famous throughout the land.

But not everyone was happy. Every song that was sung, every word that was spoken in praise of Sagbo filled his stepmother with envy. "My own son should have saved the kingdom and found favor with the king," she thought. So she grabbed Senan and handed him three palm nuts, saying, "What Sagbo has done, you can do as well. Go to the bottom of the sacred river and bring back a magic drum. The bigger, the better."

And so it was that Senan cast three palm nuts into the sacred river, jumped in after them, and swam to the bottom. There, he found the underwater village and went running toward the mansion.

The gatekeeper asked him what he was looking for and told him to go to the old woman in the house. Senan went in, saw the old woman, and told her he wanted a magic drum like the one his stepbrother had brought to their village. The woman promised to give him a magic drum, too, if he would prepare a meal for her household.

But when she gave him a single grain of corn and told him to pound it into flour, Senan burst out laughing and said mockingly, "A single grain of corn to feed a whole household! This isn't enough to feed a baby chick!" So the old woman gave him a basketful of corn. But when the meal was ready and the cooking pot and everything in the kitchen started screaming for a

share of the food, Senan went running to her. "What a stupid household you have!" he said. "Your cooking pot, your bowls, and your calabashes* — everything wants a share of the meal!"

The old woman sighed wearily and went hobbling to the kitchen, where she served everything in sight. Then she offered Senan the food that was left, but he wasn't interested in food.

"I don't want food," he said with a smirk. "I cooked the silly corn. Give me the magic drum so I can take it home right away."

So the old woman pointed to a room, saying: "Go into the room. You will find a small drum and a big drum. Take the small drum. On your return home, beat it and your wish will be fulfilled."

Senan ran into the room and grabbed the big drum instead. As he rushed out and headed for the gate, the old woman hardly had time to shout after him, "Should you run into trouble, say: 'Bees and ropes, go back where you came from.'" Senan heard and wondered what the old woman was babbling about as he hurried home with his magic drum.

His mother was overjoyed when he came back home, carrying a big drum on his head. Beaming with pride, she helped him carry the magic drum to her hut and barred the door, saying: "Now, before the whole kingdom finds out about our drum and forgets about Sagbo's, let's fill all our pots and jars with food."

But it wasn't long before Senan and his mother were heard howling and screaming for help. And men, women, and children came running from all over the village. When the door was kicked down, a murmur of astonishment ran through the crowd; for a large drum stood in the center of the hut, and Senan and his mother were tied hand and foot with ropes, while a swarm of gigantic bees swirled around them, stinging them mercilessly.

The crowd looked on, helpless. Senan rolled about on the floor and screamed until he finally remembered the old woman's parting words and shouted: "Bees and ropes, go back where you came from!" As soon as he

*calabash: gourd whose shell is used for holding liquid.

16

spoke, the bees flew out of sight, the drum melted into thin air, and the ropes binding mother and son fell to the ground.

The stepmother became a laughing stock and blamed Senan for it. Senan, too, was ashamed and tried again and again to go back to the mansion at the bottom of the sacred river, but all he found were pebbles and mud, and a few fish swimming to and fro. Of the mansion and the woman living there, he saw no further sign at all.

As for Sagbo, he grew up to be a member of the king's council and lived a long and prosperous life.

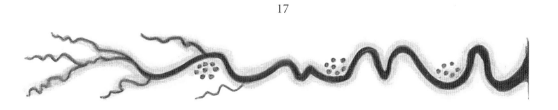

How Goat Moved from the Jungle to the Village

Haitian

One afternoon, Goat was sitting by a fire baking yams and sweet potatoes just outside his house in the jungle. He had worked very hard during the planting season and had a bumper harvest to show for it. Now that the yield of his farm had been gathered in, he was going to indulge his craving for fresh-baked yams and sweet potatoes.

As he blew on the embers and poked the fire, a plume of smoke rose and spread up into the cloudless sky. It wasn't long before the earthy, delicious smell of cooking went wafting through the jungle, carried along by the breeze. Soon the fire burned itself out and Goat, licking his lips, took a stick and quickly prodded out the big, steaming tubers of yam and sweet potato from under the ashes. Grabbing a tuber, he blew on it with all his might: "Pff…pff…pff…"

But just as he was about to bite into it, a raspy voice called out behind him: "Good afternoon."

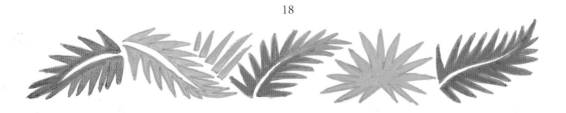

Goat jumped up and dropped the yam as though the greeting had turned it into a red-hot coal. Turning around to face the intruder, he saw Hyena standing a couple of feet away, his eyes glinting with malice.

"Good afternoon," Goat replied in a trembling voice. "You have arrived just in time for a meal. Come and help yourself to fresh-baked yams and sweet potatoes."

"I'm starving," Hyena replied, looking hungrily at Goat, "but I will eat neither yam nor sweet potato."

"I have manioc and honey-sweet corn if you don't mind waiting a few moments," Goat said, struggling to hide the fear that had come over him.

"I am really hungry," Hyena answered, "but I am not hungry for manioc or honey-sweet corn. I am hungry for you!"

Shivers coursed down Goat's spine. He wanted to run for dear life, but where could he run? He knew Hyena would always catch up with him.

"Look," Goat said, trying to talk and lie his way out of danger, "my grandfather and yours were very good friends. They were so close…"

"Shut up!" Hyena screamed, clawing the air in anger. "What do I care about your grandfather? I am hungry, not for words or friendship, but for goat meat!"

Seeing that Hyena was in no mood for talking, Goat quickly changed tactics. He took a tuber of yam and made a great show of biting into it. The yam tasted like ashes, but that didn't prevent Goat from smacking his lips. He took just a little bite at a time, but he would chew on and on. Goat was playing for time, and he was going to play for all he was worth, while looking for a way to escape from the jaws of death.

Despite his hunger, Hyena decided to wait awhile, for he wanted Goat to eat as much as possible so that he would be big enough to fill his own stomach. As Goat ate on and on, however, Hyena's patience ran out. "What is taking you so long?" he howled, stamping his feet. "I cannot wait here all evening while you go on eating. That bite will be your last, for I am starving!"

So saying, he closed in on Goat, his eyes gleaming, his claws itching to get at him.

It was then that a thunderous, blood-chilling roar sounded nearby, and Tiger came striding into view.

"Good afternoon," Tiger growled, glaring at both Hyena and Goat.

"Good afternoon," Hyena stammered, but Goat remained silent.

"Why," Tiger rumbled, fixing Goat with a fierce, inquiring gaze, "you look so glum, one would have thought you were in mourning. What's the matter with you?"

"I was about to tuck into fresh-baked yams and sweet potatoes when Hyena came by. I invited him to join in and offered to cook manioc and honey-sweet corn for him if he preferred, but he said he was going to eat me instead. I don't think he's being fair...maybe you can settle the matter."

"Whether Hyena is fair or unfair, I really cannot say," Tiger replied, glowering at Hyena with hunger in his eyes. "But it seems to me there is only one way to settle so delicate a matter. Let Goat eat his yams and sweet potatoes and let Hyena eat Goat so I can eat Hyena and settle the matter once and for all!"

Hyena felt numb all over and broke out in a sweat. He thought Tiger's solution grossly unfair, but the look in the big cat's eyes stifled the words of protest rising in his throat.

Struggling to put a brave face on the disastrous turn of events, Hyena laid his paw on Goat's neck and, shaking him, said, "Hurry up and finish your yams and sweet potatoes so I can eat you up so Tiger can eat me. But first I must step into the bush to relieve myself." So saying, Hyena disappeared into the bush.

A few moments later, Goat caught sight of Hyena running for dear life. "Your food is running away," Goat shouted to Tiger, pointing in the direction Hyena had taken. Quick as a flash, Tiger went flying through the jungle in hot pursuit.

Goat sprang to his feet and made a run for it in the opposite direction. Vowing never to return to the jungle, he headed straight for the village where he was soon joined by his parents and all his relatives. But whether Goat and his family intend to remain in the village or try their luck elsewhere remains a mystery.

The Wise Man and the Thief

Sri Lankan

Long ago, in Paduwas Nwera, there lived an old man. Appuhami was his name. In all Paduwas Nwera, there was none wiser than he. Men, women and children came from far and near to ask him questions and seek his advice. And because of his wisdom, his people appointed him village chief.

One day, a farmer named Bandayiya came to see him. On being led into Appuhami's presence, he joined his hands in a gesture of prayer and, bowing low, offered him greetings: "Long live the chief."

"The same to you," the wise man said. "What has brought you here?"

"The pursuit of truth and justice has brought me here," Bandayiya replied. "You see, someone has been stealing melons from my farm. Yesterday I saw Saroth the Thief selling melons at the marketplace. I asked him where he got them, and he told me that he had bought them from a farmer in a village nearby. I know he is lying. I know the melons are mine, but I have no way of proving it."

Bandayiya fell silent and Appuhami remained deep in thought, fixing him with a searching, meditative gaze. Then, smiling gently and leaning forward as though to lend weight to his words, he said: "Leave everything to me and do not let your heart be troubled. You shall see the truth face-to-face and justice will be done."

The wise man's words brought a sparkle to Bandayiya's eyes. Smiling broadly, he took leave of the wise man and went home rejoicing, for he knew that Appuhami's words were pure gold.

Later that evening, as Saroth sat in his hut resting from a busy day at the marketplace, he heard a voice call out a greeting and, to his surprise saw Chief Appuhami standing at his doorstep. "Long live the chief," he said quickly, jumping to his feet and bowing respectfully according to custom.

"The same to you," Appuhami replied, inclining his head slightly.

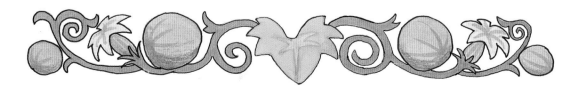

Now, a visit by the village chief was the last thing Saroth would have expected. What on earth could have prompted the chief to come to him in person? Whatever had brought him to his doorstep must be of extraordinary importance. "But what can it be?" Saroth wondered.

His heart pounded furiously as he thought of the pre-dawn trips he had made to Bandayiya's farm and all the melons he had carried off on his shoulders.

"You must be wondering why I have come to your house," Appuhami said reassuringly before Saroth could recover his tongue. "A matter of great urgency has been brought before me, a matter demanding the attention of anybody of standing in our village. You are a very important member of this community. Tomorrow morning there will be a special village meeting to consider the matter. Something tells me that you will be the man of the hour, the one on whose valuable opinion the success or failure of our gathering will depend."

No sooner had Appuhami taken leave of Saroth than the voice of the chief's messenger and the sound of his drum shook the still evening air: "The chief is inviting the whole village to a meeting to discuss an extraordinary matter tomorrow morning. Everybody is invited, especially anybody of importance."

Saroth stood listening for a moment, tongue-tied with amazement. To think that the message now being drummed to the multitude had been delivered to him personally by the chief himself! To him who people called thief behind his back! He would treasure forever the moment when he heard with his own ears Appuhami tell him that he was somebody and that his opinion would make or break the outcome of the gathering!

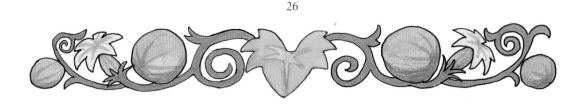

"Is this a dream I am having?" he wondered again and again. "But how can it be? I have seen Appuhami with my own eyes and heard him with my own ears. And the drum of Appuhami's messenger, isn't it still booming Appuhami's message to the four corners of the village this very moment?"

Saroth's head swelled with pride and his spine tingled with excitement as the chief's words echoed and re-echoed in his ears: "You are a very important member of this community, the one on whose valuable opinion the success or failure of our gathering will depend."

Quickly Saroth got dressed and flew out of his hut to tell the whole village how the chief had come to him in person and what he had come to tell him. Saroth went from house to house, boasting about Appuhami's visit and the words he had spoken:

He came to see me in my house, Appuhami the great chief!
Me who so many people have accused of being a thief!
And he told me that in his view I was a man of great power!
For the urgent matter at hand, I'll be the man of the hour!

It did not matter that wherever Saroth went people gave him strange looks and whispered to each other as though what he told them were the ravings of a lunatic. The more people whispered to each other, the greater his resolve to make them agree with the chief's impression of him.

The next morning, Saroth went forth to the meeting place, stepping proudly as though he was going to preside over the gathering. As was the custom, he was stripped to the waist, but that was to his advantage, for Saroth was a fine figure of a man. He was well-proportioned, with broad shoulders, the torso of a weightlifter and strong, powerful legs.

The arena where the meeting was to be held was packed with people when Saroth got there, but Appuhami had saved a space for him in the front row. A hush fell on the gathering when Appuhami raised his hand for silence.

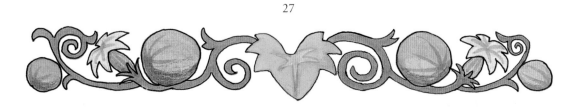

"I called this meeting," he said, "because a very important matter has been brought to me. Someone has been stealing melons from Bandayiya's farm, and we must find the culprit. Bandayiya usually sprinkles ashes over his melons. The thief must therefore have ashes on his shoulders from carrying the fruit. I am going to take a close look around. Anyone found to have ashes on his shoulders will have to explain to the village how they got there."

Saroth's hands instinctively flew to his shoulders, wiping them with a few quick strokes of the fingers. The tell-tale gesture lasted no more than a fraction of a moment, but everyone saw it, for at Appuhami's mention of the theft of Bandayiya's melons, all eyes turned to Saroth.

"Saroth is the one who stole Bandayiya's melons," Appuhami said, slowly.

"I did not!" cried Saroth. "I am not a thief!"

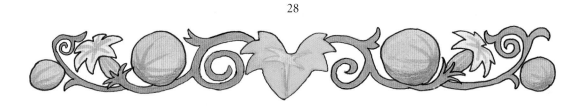

But when Appuhami asked him what had made him wipe his shoulders, his tongue failed him and the words stuck in his throat.

"Your gesture has given you away," said Appuhami. "A man who has eaten hot pepper may deny it, but the shooing sound of the wind he sucks in to cool his mouth will surely give him away."

All the villagers agreed that Saroth's gesture was indeed an admission of guilt. He was made to pay for the melons he had stolen and to endure for a whole day the ordeal of *dadu kade gahanawa**, the traditional punishment for theft and other breaches of the law.

In proving Saroth's guilt, Appuhami earned among his people a reputation as the wisest man ever to have walked this earth. And nothing has made them change their minds since.

* *dadu kade gahanawa*: an old instrument to punish criminals, similar to the stocks.

29

Anansi and the Guinea Bird

Antiguan

The land had fallen on hard times. A drought like no other in living memory had parched the grass and the trees and laid bare the bed of the mighty river that provided water for the village. Anansi's last reserves had run out and he knew he must find a way to fill his belly or die a miserable death. What could he do? Anansi thought long and hard but he could find no answer. Then an idea occurred to him and his face lit up with a smile: he was going to ask the Sky God to make a new law.

"The world would be a better place if people did not spend their lives nosing around, meddling in their neighbors' business," Anansi told the Sky God. "Let anyone who does not mind their own business simply drop down dead." The Sky God considered Anansi's words and they found favor with him.

Pleased with this new state of affairs, Anansi immediately set out to make a garden on the rocky hillside. He got out his garden tools — a hoe, a

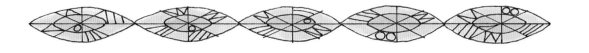

machete and a pickax — and he started to pick away at the rock, pretending he was cultivating his garden.

Soon Goat came walking by. "What is Anansi up to?" he wondered aloud, his eyes widening in bewilderment. "Trying to grow food on a rock?" Instantly he dropped down dead on the spot. Quickly Anansi took Goat to his house and, for the first time in a long while, he had a good meal. "Well," he said, belching noisily, "wherever you are, I hope you have learned your lesson, Goat. Think twice before meddling in other people's business!"

The next day, Anansi returned to his garden and once again made a big show of chipping away at the rock. Soon Pig came by, and he, too, was amazed to see Anansi bent double and striking at the rock with his pickax.

"Anansi!" he grunted. "Trying to grow food from stone! Surely you know better than that!" And like Goat before him, Pig dropped down dead on the spot.

As the days went by, a great many creatures suffered the same plight: Buffalo, Lion, Vulture, Elephant, Parrot, Hyena — they all fell for Anansi's deadly trick and ended up in his bottomless pit of a stomach.

So while the whole land was starving, Anansi grew plump and fleshy, for he had an endless supply of meat in his house. And he would have eaten birds and beasts alike to extinction if Guinea Bird had not spied on Anansi and decided to turn his own trickery against him.

Now Guinea Bird was almost completely bald with just a few feathers on the top of his head. He found himself a horse and saddle and made a song which he practiced for weeks in preparation for his encounter with the wily Anansi.

And so it was that one morning, while Anansi was chipping away at the rock in his garden, Guinea Bird came riding by, singing at the top of his voice: "All them boy who go a' barber shop part them hair like me!"

Guinea Bird rode past Anansi in one direction, then turned around and rode past him again in the opposite direction. And as he rode up and down, he kept tossing his bald head and singing: "All them boy who go a' barber shop part them hair like me!"

Anansi was speechless. "What kind of nonsense is this?" he snorted, as he watched Guinea Bird majestically riding his horse, turning his bald head this way and that, and passing his wing over it proudly. Struggling to keep his self-control, Anansi went on chipping away at the rock in his garden. But Guinea Bird kept riding up and down the path by Anansi's garden, singing all the while.

33

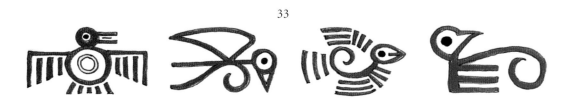

34

Anansi found it increasingly difficult to go on working, but he did his best to ignore Guinea Bird and his silly song. Finally he stopped working and, leaning on his pickax, simply watched Guinea Bird all morning, hoping he would lose his voice and leave him alone.

But Guinea Bird went on singing as loudly as ever. What was Anansi to do? He tried not to lose patience, but that was as hard as keeping one's fingers from scratching an itchy spot. Anansi ground his teeth to stop himself from speaking, and when that didn't work he bit his tongue, and when that didn't work he closed his eyes, hoping that Guinea Bird would go away and his song fade into silence. But it was all in vain.

Finally Anansi looked up to the heavens and said, "Sky God, it was I who got you to make this law, but I must ask you. What does Guinea Bird have on his head to part?" And no sooner had those words crossed his lips than he dropped down dead.

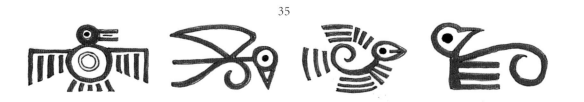

A Fisherman and His Dog

Puerto Rican

There once lived in San Juan an old fisherman, Don Manolito by name. Tall and spare, with a head full of graying, silvery hair and a childlike, melancholy smile, Don Manolito lived in a little hut at the edge of town. No one really knew how he came to settle in San Juan. Some people said he had come from a remote part of the island, sorrowful and broken-hearted after the death of his beloved wife. Others said that he was a member of the Spanish royal family who had come to San Juan seeking a simple, peaceful life.

A man of few words, Don Manolito was kind and friendly, but he had no close friend except for his dog, Taino, who was a quiet, gentle creature with glistening black hair and long, pointed ears. Whether Don Manolito was going to the marketplace or running errands, Taino always kept him company, trotting at his heels or walking by his side, his ears perked up, his tongue lolling out. Whenever a visitor came to their hut, Taino would sit at Don Manolito's feet, a silent listener to their conversation.

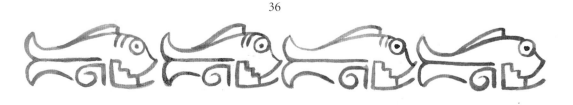

Now, Don Manolito used to go fishing several days a week and never was he known to set sail without Taino walking with him to the edge of the sea. There Taino would remain until Don Manolito came rowing his boat ashore in the evening. Don Manolito never failed to save the best of the catch for their evening meal. And Taino always looked forward to the moment when the delicious smell of steaming, sizzling fish tickled his nose as it issued forth from their hut and went floating through the air. Anyone who crossed their doorstep at that moment was sure to get a warm welcome and a good meal.

For the townsfolk of San Juan, the sight of Don Manolito and Taino setting out for the seashore in the morning and coming back in the evening, and the delicious smell of food which followed their return became a ritual, a part of the natural rhythm and pattern of things: the ebb and flow of the ocean, sunrise and sunset, the waxing and waning of the moon.

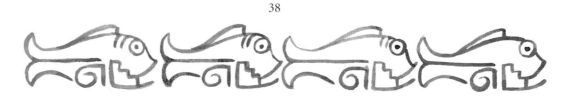

One morning, shortly after Don Manolito's boat had vanished from sight, the sky gradually covered itself with dark clouds. As the sun grew dimmer and dimmer and the wind gathered strength, the stillness was shaken now and then by the rumbling of distant thunder. People hurried to and fro on urgent errands before retreating to the safety of their homes. Fishermen came rowing furiously ashore, bringing tales of a storm raging fiercely at sea.

In no time at all the seashore was deserted, except for Taino. As the thunder rumbled louder and the sky grew darker, Taino sat patiently on his haunches and looked out to sea, waiting for Don Manolito to come rowing his boat ashore. But of Don Manolito or his rowing boat there was neither sight nor sound.

While Taino waited, the storm burst in on the town with flashes of lightning and peals of thunder. And the sea roared in response, sending towering waves crashing upon the shore. Taino was swept off his feet again

and again as the waves rushed upon him. Finally he threw himself into the sea and swam all the way to a rock jutting out of the roaring waters. The storm raged all evening and far into the night. The din of the rolling thunder as it merged with the crash of the waves upon the shore made many a brave man's blood run cold.

Taino kept his vigil, sitting high on the rock jutting out of the stormy waters. Hour after hour, he sat there on his haunches, looking out to sea and waiting for Don Manolito to come rowing his boat ashore. But of Don Manolito or his rowing boat, there was neither sight nor sound.

As night slowly brightened into dawn, the storm subsided and the roll of thunder grew ever more distant until it was heard no more. The wrath of the sea was stilled and, all over San Juan, life resumed its course. Yet high on the rock above the waters, Taino remained sitting on his haunches, looking out to sea and waiting for Don Manolito to come rowing his boat ashore. But of Don Manolito or his rowing boat there was neither sight nor sound.

Suddenly someone pointed at the rock and a shout went up, followed by another and another until, from one end of the shore to the other, exclamations of amazement and wonder rose to the heavens. Quickly the fishermen jumped into their boats and rowed as fast as they could toward the rock.

"Why, it's Taino!" cried a fisherman who had rowed ahead of the rest. And soon all were crying, "It's Taino! It's Taino!" But why and how Taino came to be on that rock was a mystery none could fathom.

Then it came to them that Don Manolito had not been seen since rowing out to sea the day before and that Taino had been sitting on that rock throughout the storm and through the night, waiting for his friend. A chill ran down their spines and they all fell silent, for they knew then that Don Manolito had been caught in the terrible storm and would never come back.

"Let's take Taino back to shore, for he must be cold and hungry," said one of the fishermen as he clambered onto the rock. But when he laid his hands on the dog to pick him up, he cried out in surprise and dismay. Taino had turned to stone!

The sad tidings of Taino's transformation swept through San Juan and the whole island, and a great fear came upon the people, for they took it to be a sign foreshadowing the end of Time itself. Some said that the sun would drop out of the heavens any moment, burning the earth to ashes. Some said that the sea was about to rise up and sweep all of them into the deep. And others said that the earth was going to open up and swallow the whole world.

40

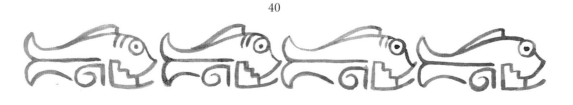

For many days, men, women, and children lived in fear. But then the days lengthened into weeks, and weeks into months, and no catastrophe overwhelmed the people of San Juan. The sun did not drop out of the heavens, the sea did not overflow its bounds, nor did the earth split open. Once again the shore of the sea echoed to the voices of fishermen rowing out to sea or bringing their boats ashore, of men and women haggling over fish, and of youngsters and children at play. And all over San Juan, fear of apocalypse was swept up in the rough and tumble of daily living, overtaken by the natural rhythm and pattern of things: the ebb and flow of the ocean, sunrise and sunset, the waxing and waning of the moon.

The men and women who knew Taino and Don Manolito in the flesh, and who lived through those fear-laden days when the earth's final hour seemed to be at hand, have long gone out of this world into the Great Beyond. Memory of the storm which overwhelmed Don Manolito at sea is lost in the mists of time, and San Juan has grown into a bustling metropolis. But on a rock off the coast of the modern city, near the rush and roar of traffic, a dog of stone still sits on its haunches, looking out to sea in silent witness to the greatest friendship ever to have united a fisherman and his dog.

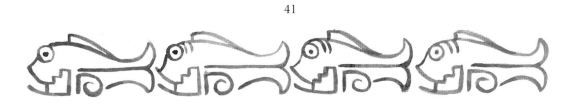

Why Cat and Dog Do Not Get Along

Cape Verdean

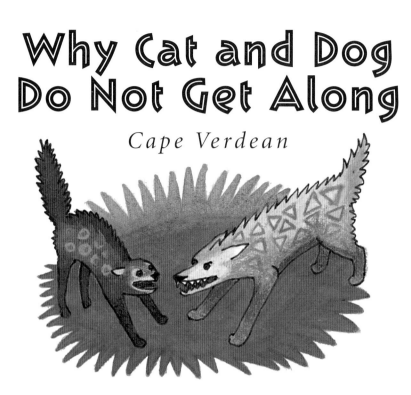

Long ago, when the world was new, Cat and Dog were friends. In the village where they lived, no friendship had ever lasted for so long, nor excited so much envy and admiration. They gathered food together, they ate together, and they stored their reserves together. Wherever one went, the other would go too. They watched out for each other and took care of each other, like brothers. Nothing and nobody, it seemed, could bring enmity between the two friends.

It came to pass, however, that their village was stricken by famine and, like everyone else, Cat and Dog had great difficulty finding food. One day they could find nothing to eat. They searched and searched, but they found no food.

"What on earth are we going to do?" Cat mewed.

"I don't know," Dog whimpered, "but we have no choice but to go on searching." And so they did.

Suddenly the delicious smell of fresh homemade cheese came floating to them on the evening air, tickling their nostrils and making their stomachs burn with hunger. For a few restless moments, the two companions lifted up their heads and, sniffing hungrily, sent their eyes roving over the whole village.

It wasn't long before they were making their way toward a hut with wisps of smoke drifting over its roof. The two friends exchanged knowing looks and whispered together briefly. Drawing apart, Cat took cover on one side, near the entrance to the hut, while Dog made a great racket around the back, jumping up and down, barking and yelping as though to warn the owners of the hut of approaching danger.

Soon a man and a woman came out of the hut and ran around the back.

As they stood and watched, wondering at the meaning of the alarm the strange dog had sounded, Cat dashed into the hut and made off with a large piece of the homemade cheese.

But when Dog finally rejoined his friend, they could not agree on how to share the piece of cheese.

"To make sure each of us gets an equal share of the cheese, let's call on Donkey for help," Dog panted. "He is a creature of few words, but he is fair-minded."

"Fair-minded, indeed!" Cat replied. "The fellow is so stupid he hardly knows his own mind. Who has ever heard of a donkey helping to settle anything? I would rather call on Goat. There is a righteous fellow, and his beard is surely a sign of wisdom."

"Don't be silly!" Dog growled. "That stinking devil will make the food smell and spoil my appetite!"

The two friends argued on and on, with no compromise in sight, for whatever one put forward the other was sure to find fault with.

But then, in the heat of the argument, Monkey's name came up and the two companions quickly agreed that he would indeed make a wise judge. And so it was that they hurried to Monkey's house.

"What good wind has blown you here?" Monkey cried as he saw Cat and Dog walk into his compound. "It has been a long time since I…"

Catching sight of the cheese the visitors had brought with them, he broke off in mid-sentence, licking his lips greedily.

"We need to know how to share this cheese equally," Cat and Dog shouted, holding the stolen food out to Monkey. "Only you can help us."

"With pleasure," Monkey replied, his eyes bright with cunning. "This is something I do every day, even for total strangers, and I will gladly do it for you, my dear friends."

Monkey sent for a knife and a set of scales, but instead of cutting the cheese into halves, he made one piece larger than the other.

"This isn't right," Monkey cried, shaking his head in feigned disappointment as he weighed the two parts in the scales. "This isn't right at all!" Quickly he bit off part of the heavier piece and ate it as Cat and Dog watched in astonishment. But Monkey had bitten off so much that what was the heavier part was now the lighter part. "What have I done?" Monkey moaned, holding his head with both hands. "I am not myself today." To even things up, he bit a chunk off the other piece.

Seeing that the cheese they had brought was now half gone, Cat and Dog sprang to their feet and demanded: "Give us what is left of the cheese so we can share it between ourselves."

"No," said Monkey, chewing greedily, "I hate to do things by halves. I must preserve my reputation for wisdom and keep the peace between the two of you."

Cat and Dog lunged at Monkey, but he quickly sprang clear and, clutching the remainder of the cheese in one hand, scrambled up a tree and vanished from sight.

Cat and Dog then turned on each other, eyes blazing and teeth flashing. "You must pay for this. Monkey was your choice," Cat screeched.

"Not me! You said Monkey would make a good judge," Dog howled.

"No, not me — you!"

"No, not me — you!"

And the two friends fell on each other, scratching and biting and hissing and screaming.

From that day to this, Cat and Dog have borne a grudge against each other. Even when they seem to have made peace once more, the old quarrel is still there, lying just beneath the surface, waiting to flare up at any moment.

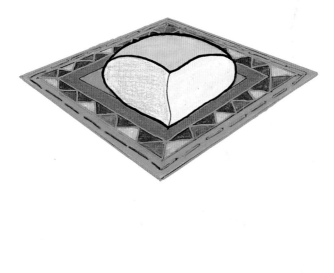

The Call of the Eagle

Malaysian

Once upon a time, in a little village by the sea, there lived a boy named
Si-Tangang and his widowed mother. Si-Tangang was still a baby when his
father died, yet a happier, more carefree child never walked the earth, for
Si-Tangang's mother was the best mother under the sun. When he was a
baby, she made up enchanting lullabies for him and, as he grew older, she
prepared delicious meals for him — rice with fried fish-eggs, grilled chicken,
beans and beef curry, yam cakes and dried banana chips.

Her love for Si-Tangang knew no bounds and Si-Tangang brought her
great joy in return, for he was radiant with health, handsome, quick-witted,
affectionate and well behaved. While the other children were playing,
Si-Tangang helped his mother in their rice paddy. He kept her well supplied
with water and firewood, and washed her clothes as well as his own.

Every night Si-Tangang's mother told him stories — fairy tales, animal
and ghost stories and, above all, tales of the sea. She was a captivating story-

48

teller and her tales of brave captains sailing the seven seas and defending their treasure-laden ships against pirates set his imagination on fire.

He often accompanied her to the marketplace and on her various errands in the village, but the seashore was his favorite place; for while his mother was haggling with fishermen over the price of fish and shrimp, Si-Tangang would steal away to a quiet spot on the beach and gaze dreamily at the distant ships majestically ploughing their way across the sea, their sails flapping in the breeze. And as he sat there, he would sometimes picture himself commanding a magnificent ship bound on a voyage to the ends of the earth, where fame and fortune awaited him. But whenever he shared these visions with his mother, she would point out the dangers — sharks, storms, pirates and shipwrecks — and urge him to lead a peaceful life as a farmer, teacher or merchant.

Time passed, Si-Tangang grew to early manhood, and his longing to roam the seas became ever stronger. "I will be a captain," he whispered to himself one day as he stood gazing out to sea. "I will be a captain, for only then can I satisfy the cravings of my heart."

As soon as he got back that day, he told his mother of his decision. She bowed her head and remained silent for a long time. When at last she spoke, there was no mistaking her strength of feeling: "Si-Tangang, my son, my only hope! Losing you is worse than death to me!"

To that Si-Tangang replied: "Though I am fated to sail to the ends of the earth, I will always hold you close to my heart. I will bring you joy, not sorrow, and great good fortune."

His mother pleaded passionately for him to stay. "The life of a seaman is a fickle, uncertain thing full of hardship and danger," she argued. "Think of the storms, the fierce beasts of the deep. Think of the mountains of ice lurking beneath the surface, the rocks veiled in mist. Think of the pirates bent on violence and loot. Think also of being parted from your loved ones. Think, think again before you commit yourself to a choice that may bring grief to you and me."

His mother's plea shook Si-Tangang to the core. Never before had she stood up to him with such power and passion, and he had a feeling the world was tumbling about his ears. For a long time, Si-Tangang was torn between obedience to his mother and to his own indomitable will. But in the end, he stood by his decision, and his mother had to let him go.

And so it was that Si-Tangang became a sailor. He traveled the world and was well liked by all who worked with him. Not a day went by without Si-Tangang thinking about his mother and he never missed a chance to send her news of himself along with presents — magnificent jewelry, sparkling gems and rich, exotic clothing.

But one day his ship was set upon by pirates, and the captain was murdered. The rest of the crew were about to give themselves up, when Si-Tangang sprang to the fore. Strengthening his shipmates' flagging courage, he led them in a fierce battle against the attackers. The pirates were finally driven off, and the ship resumed her voyage with Si-Tangang as her captain.

Si-Tangang's heroic victory over the pirates made him the idol of seamen the world over. In his native village, his exploits were celebrated in stories and songs. His childhood friends, his relatives, indeed all who knew him, stood taller in the dazzling radiance of Si-Tangang's name; but no one stood taller than his mother, the one who was in regular contact with him and who had a thousand precious gifts as proof of his love for her.

Within a year of becoming a captain, Si-Tangang fell in love and married a beautiful princess from the rich and powerful kingdom of Siam. But from the moment that Si-Tangang told his bride about his mother, she took a dislike to her. "I cannot possibly put up with such a low-born wretch for a mother-in-law," she muttered darkly to herself. "I will not rest until I make Si-Tangang turn away from her in shame!"

So when Si-Tangang told her of his desire to sail back to his native village to see his mother, she whispered, "That woman you call mother, my love, cannot be your real mother. You are of noble birth. A great prince can only claim descent from a powerful queen. Your true mother must have been someone else."

Si-Tangang was deeply troubled and told his wife in reply, "She may be low-born, poor and powerless, but my beloved mother is dearer to me than fame and fortune!"

To that, Si-Tangang's wife could find nothing to say but, deep in her heart, the resolve to poison her husband's mind against his mother remained as strong as ever.

Day followed day, weeks lengthened into months and months turned into years. Si-Tangang still yearned to see his mother. But whenever he decided to set a date for the voyage back to his native village, the words of his wife would echo in his ears.

In the meantime, not a word did he send to his mother, and the presents he had bought for her were left to gather dust in a remote corner of his mansion.

But one night Si-Tangang had a dream: his mother was holding out to him a dish heaped with steaming rice and fried fish-eggs. Si-Tangang was very hungry and the food smelled delicious, but his wife would not let him eat it. "If you take the food from that shabby old woman," she taunted, "your name will forever be covered in shame." So Si-Tangang turned away from his mother and refused to eat in spite of the hunger tearing at his stomach. Weeping and wailing, his mother threw herself at his knees and would not let him go.

Si-Tangang woke with a start, his heart pounding, and for the first time since his wedding, the words his mother had spoken the day he left her rang in his ears: "Si-Tangang, my son, my only hope! Losing you is worse than death to me!"

That day Si-Tangang told his wife they must prepare for a voyage to his native village to see his mother.

Soon he and the princess set sail, together with numerous members of the royal family, several distinguished guests and many priceless gifts for Si-Tangang's mother. For days, Si-Tangang's majestic ship ploughed her way across the wide, boundless sea, her bright sail fluttering in the wind. As she drew closer and closer to his native village, Si-Tangang wondered whether the time was right for a reunion with his mother. She must have grown old

and gray by now. What would his guests say when they saw him embrace a poor, shabby woman worn down with age?

Si-Tangang's wife saw the shadow of doubt that had crept over his face, and her face beamed with malicious joy. But when the shore of Si-Tangang's native village came into view, a great fear gripped the princess, for there was no telling what Si-Tangang was going to do. Si-Tangang, she knew, still loved his mother, even if the poison of doubt had started to sink in. As the ship dropped anchor, the princess made a final attempt to sever once and for all the bond between mother and son: "That woman you call mother, my love, cannot be your real mother. You are of noble birth. A great prince can only claim descent from a powerful queen. Your true mother must have been someone else."

As Si-Tangang stood gazing at his wife's tearful face, there came to him a vision of himself hugging his mother, a shabby, shapeless woman hoary with age, while a crowd of men, women and children were pointing at him, sneering and taunting. Then his mind curdled. "That woman is no part of me," he muttered to himself, clenching his teeth. "That woman is no part of me."

For three days, Si-Tangang's ship stood motionless, for Si-Tangang was neither willing to go ashore and be reunited with his mother, nor able to give the order for departure. In the meantime, news of his arrival had spread through the village and far beyond. Si-Tangang's mother and all the villagers waited and waited for him to come ashore, but there was neither sight nor sound of him.

"What on earth is holding him back from coming home to me?" she wondered. "If he will not come to me, what is to keep me from going to him?" she said finally as she packed dishes of rice and fried fish-eggs and grilled chicken into a boat, and rowed toward Si-Tangang's ship under a sky hanging low with brooding storm clouds.

She climbed aboard, calling Si-Tangang by name and balancing on her head a tray of her son's favorite dishes. When at last she found him, she set the food-laden tray down and hobbled toward him, arms outstretched and crying: "Si-Tangang, my son, what has held you back from rowing ashore and coming home to me?"

Si-Tangang saw that she was old and had lost most of her teeth, and her skin was wrinkled and sagging. He stepped back, his face darkening with shame and anger. "Do not touch me!" he screamed. "You are no part of me!"

"Why, you are out of your mind, Si-Tangang, my son. I am your beloved mother and I have come to welcome you back home," she said, laying her hands on his shoulders.

As all on board looked on, Si-Tangang stepped back from his mother and replied coldly: "I am a prince, and you are a low-born wreck of a woman. How dare you call me son!"

Weeping and wailing, Si-Tangang's mother clambered down from the ship into her boat. "I come to my son, flesh of my flesh and bone of my bone, and he says he is no part of me! May God, from whose sight nothing is ever hidden, be the judge! In sorrow, not in anger, do I call on you, O Lord, for you alone know which of us is true and which is false."

No sooner had she rowed back ashore than there was a deafening clap of thunder and Si-Tangang, who seemed to have gone into a trance, was startled back into consciousness. "What have I done?" he cried, holding his head in both hands. "What have I done? I have done a foul, unspeakable deed! A most foul, unspeakable deed!" The princess tried to hush Si-Tangang's lamentations, but he pushed past her and ran to the side of the ship, calling after his mother.

Then Si-Tangang's body started to change. Feathers grew on his back and chest, his arms turned into wings, his mouth lengthened into a beak, his feet withered and his toes became claws. Si-Tangang had turned into an eagle! While his wife and all on board fell back in horror, he flew away from the ship, calling ma! ma! a heart-rending plea for forgiveness. As he circled over

his mother's house, calling ma! ma! all the while, his ship suddenly capsized and sank, with everything in it, down to the ocean floor.

Every day Si-Tangang continued to circle over his mother's house, still calling and begging for forgiveness — ma! ma! His mother heard him, and broke down and wept, for the forgiveness he asked was not hers to grant but God's.

To the end of her life, Si-Tangang's mother went on weeping, for every morning she awoke to the call of the eagle and every night she went to sleep with the call of the eagle ringing in her ears.

The call of the eagle has sounded through the ages, and will continue to do so to remind us of what Si-Tangang did to his mother and how he tried to atone for it.

Leopard's Argument with Monkey

Zaïrian

Once upon a time, Leopard woke from sleep and set out from his den in search of food. The sun had just lifted its face above the rim of the horizon, flooding the heavens with light. The green grass glistened with dewdrops, and the forest was alive with birdsong and the cries of a thousand creatures.

Leopard lay in wait for a long time, crouching on all fours, his ears pricked, ready to spring out for the kill, but neither antelope, nor buffalo, nor any other creature wandered within range.

As Leopard waited, a great flaming anger came over him. "How long will I have to wait before I get something to eat?" he growled. "The way things are going, I might wait a whole day and not have a rat to show for it!" And he went tearing through the forest, his sharp teeth glinting like rows of shiny knives held up to the sun. But then there was a mighty crash and Leopard was heard howling to be rescued. "Help! Help! I have fallen into a well. Pull me out, somebody! Pull me out before I die. Pull me out, plea-ea-ea-ea-se!"

The well into which Leopard had plunged lay a short distance from a clump of trees where monkeys were at play. Some were hanging from the leafy branches by their feet, some were swinging from one tree to another, and some were racing each other to the top of the tallest trees and back. There was a general panic when the howls of the hunter burst in upon their happy hour, and they vanished like fairies at the crack of dawn.

They remained hidden from view for a long time while Leopard went on howling and pleading for someone to pull him out of the well. Then, realizing that they were in no immediate danger, the monkeys came out of hiding and started creeping cautiously toward the well.

Finally, their leader, the tallest and strongest of them, stepped boldly to the rim of the well and looked in. "The fellow is in trouble all right!" he said, looking around at the other monkeys, a spiteful smile on his face. At this, they all rushed forward and soon the well was surrounded by a crowd of monkeys jostling for a good look at the deadly enemy now at their mercy.

From the bottom of the well, Leopard pleaded as best he could:

Pull me out, gentle monkeys! Please do not let me die.
I give a solemn promise, which I will ever stand by;
Save, save me now and we shall be friends for life.
No longer will my kind and your kind be at strife!

"No one will help you get out of that well!" one monkey cried. "You have waged war on us since the days of our ancestors. You have never shown us any mercy. Why should we show you mercy now?"

And the leader added:

Plead until nightfall and you shall have pleaded in vain;
There at the bottom of the well you shall remain.
To me and my kind you have brought terror and death.
We'll not be safe from danger so long as you have breath.

The monkeys ignored the hunter's pleas for help. Yet Leopard kept begging for mercy, hoping beyond hope that they to whom he had brought nothing but fear and death would be moved to pity and save his life. He went on pleading until his voice grew faint. And when his voice had grown so weak they could barely hear him, the monkeys drifted away, knowing full well that their enemy had but a little time left to live.

But one of them could not quite bring himself to leave, for he was torn between hate for the hunter and pity for the hunter's cruel fate. Stooping over the rim of the well, he looked down at Leopard and spoke:

Do you really mean it — what I heard you say:
Never again will you seek and hunt us for your prey
If we take pity, trust what you say, and save your life,
There will at last be peace between us, an end to strife?

And the hunter replied with all the strength he could muster:

As you and all the others have heard,
I have pledged my most solemn word.
If you should take pity and save my life,
There will be an end to enmity and strife.

The monkey stepped back and went into a bush nearby. It was not long before he came back holding a rope. "May your word be your bond," he sighed as he lowered the rope into the well.

Quickly Leopard grabbed it and began his climb while Monkey tugged and strained to keep his balance. Before long Leopard emerged from the well, but no sooner had he touched the ground than he grabbed his savior by the tail, his eyes burning like fire, his claws sticking out like the quills of a porcupine fighting for its life.

"You're hurting me!" Monkey cried, trying to wriggle his tail free from Leopard's grasp.

"Hurting you!" Leopard growled. "I am going to eat you, for I am very hungry."

"How can you treat me so?" Monkey screamed. "Only a moment ago, you spoke words of peace and friendship. Let me go, for you have given me your word!"

But Leopard replied:

My words have as much substance as the breeze
Blowing yonder among the tall and leafy trees.
Born to love blood and fresh, juicy meat,
I cannot let my promise stop my need to eat!

Monkey scolded Leopard for being such a cheat, demanding that he let go of him at once. But Leopard was determined not to let go; it was his right as a hunter to catch and eat monkeys!

The two of them were still locked in a battle of words when Tortoise, who happened to be passing by, asked why they were arguing so loudly.

"I really don't understand this at all!" Tortoise exclaimed after both Leopard and Monkey had each told their side of the story. "Am I to believe that Monkey has enough strength in his arms to pull Leopard out of a well as deep as this?" he sneered, shaking his head in disbelief. "Tell me another joke — I'm not such a fool as I look."

"But I did pull him out of the well, and my hands are still hurting from the strain of it," cried Monkey, holding his hands up for Tortoise to see.

"You may argue as much as you like, but I won't believe either of you until I see this thing with my own eyes!" said Tortoise.

"Let it never be said that I told a lie," Leopard growled, letting go of Monkey's tail. "Let's do it again so he can see the truth with his own eyes."

So saying, Leopard jumped back into the well. Tortoise peered down after him to make sure Leopard had reached the bottom. Then he nodded several times and, turning to face Monkey, waved good-bye to him and ambled off toward the setting sun.

"Farewell!" Monkey cried and went off in the opposite direction.

At the bottom of the well, Leopard waited and waited for Monkey to pull him out so he could clear his name and eat his fill of monkey meat. Some say that Leopard is still waiting at the bottom of that well, wondering why Monkey has kept him waiting all these years.

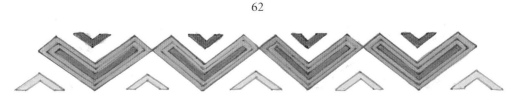

Sources

THE MAGIC DRUM — *Beninese*

I recorded and translated this story as part of my Beninese folk-tale preservation project. It is a story from the Fon, the largest ethnic group in the republic of Benin. The story dramatizes the importance of kindness, respect for the elderly and the need to keep one's tongue under control. The story also illustrates the significance of the drum in African culture.

HOW GOAT MOVED FROM THE JUNGLE TO THE VILLAGE — *Haitian*

This story was told to me by a seventy-five-year-old man from Haiti named Joseph Eliné Jacques. He spoke in Creole and his son, Robert Jacques, a close friend of mine, translated his words into English. The presence of a hyena in the story points to its African origin. This story is an interesting variant of the parable of the unmerciful servant (Matthew 18:23-35).

THE WISE MAN AND THE THIEF — *Sri Lankan*

I was told this trickster tale by Mr. Simpath Sembapperuma. The story was one of those his grandmother told him when he was a child. The figure of the village chief, called "Gamarala," is a common character in Sri Lankan folklore.

ANANSI AND THE GUINEA BIRD — *Antiguan*

This story was given to me by Dr. Althea Prince, an award-winning writer and storyteller whom I befriended soon after I started working on *The Barefoot Book of Tropical Tales*. "Anansi and the Guinea Bird" is one of the innumerable stories her mother told her. Anansi is the traditional trickster figure in the folklore of most Caribbean countries, but Ghana is his native country.

A FISHERMAN AND HIS DOG — *Puerto Rican*

This is the legend surrounding a rock shaped like a dog rising out of the sea off the coast of San Juan. The story was first told to me by Mrs. Linda Garcia, a native of Puerto Rico. Most of the Puerto Ricans I discussed the story with were familiar with it, but only one had actually seen the rock, a woman called Catina Caban-Owen, who told me that her father had shown her the rock and told her the story behind it. Having seen the rock several times and remembering it clearly, she was very valuable in helping me to build up a mental picture of the rock, and ultimately in fleshing out the story. The closest variant to this tale is, perhaps, Ovid's story of Niobe's transformation into stone through grief.

The name I gave the dog is charged with symbolic significance. "Taino" is the name of a pre-Colombian Indian tribe living in Puerto Rico. In choosing that name, I wanted to make the friendship between the dog and Don Manolito, immortalized in the legend of the rock off the coast of San Juan, an emblem of the island's multiracial and multicultural identity.

WHY CAT AND DOG DO NOT GET ALONG — *Cape Verdean*

This story is an adaptation of "Dividing the Cheese," a folk tale published in *Folk Tales of All Nations*, edited by F. H. Lee, Tudor Publishing Company, New York, 1936. In the original story, two cats are the antagonists. By making them a cat and a dog in my version, the story is transformed into a "Pourquoi" tale, explaining why cats and dogs don't get along.

THE CALL OF THE EAGLE — *Malaysian*

This metamorphosis story from Malaysia calls to mind many stories from Ovid's *Metamorphoses*, such as the story of the transformation of Tereus, his wife Procne and her sister Philomela into birds. I was told this story by a charming Malaysian woman named Normah Khairudhin and her beautiful daughter Siti Khairudhin. This story dramatizes a belief enshrined in Malaysian culture: a mother is sacred.

LEOPARD'S ARGUMENT WITH MONKEY — *Zaïrian*

This story is an adaptation of Kama Kamanda's "Le Guépard et la Guenon" ("The Cheetah and the Monkey"), one of the stories in *Les Contes Veillées Africaines*, Editions L'Harmattan, Paris, 1995. Whereas the original story has two main characters, a cheetah and a monkey, mine has three characters, a monkey, a leopard and a tortoise. Here, Tortoise is the trickster, a role he sometimes plays in African folk tales.

ACKNOWLEDGMENTS

The debt of gratitude I incurred while working on *The Barefoot Book of Tropical Tales* is beyond measure, and naming everyone to whom I am indebted is an impossible task. But among these, there are some without whose help and support this book could not have been written, and I want to single them out for acknowledgment.

My thanks go to my wife Cherifa and our children, Farida, Rabiath, Gemilath, Raman and Rahim, for their patience and understanding.

I am also thankful to the late Mr. Richard Walker, to Ms. Tessa Strickland, Ms. Fran Parnell, Ms. Mary Finch and Ms. Kate Parker for everything they have done to bring this book into being. Many thanks to Mr. Eshu Lawrence Bumpus, Mr. Xiong Leng, Dr. Sonia Cintron-Marrero, Dr. Barbara Molette, Ms. Earna Luering, Dr. Celia Anderson, Professor Imna Arroyo, Dr. Abdul Khaleque, Dr. Lee Haring and Dr. Donez Xiques. I am equally grateful to Dr. David Carter, Dr. Dimitrios Pachis, Dr. Stanley Battle as well as the Connecticut State University System and Eastern Connecticut State University. I also want to express my gratitude to all of my teachers in Benin, England, Togo, France and the USA.

Finally, my thanks go forth to all the native storytellers and informants whose voices were my primary guides in setting down in writing the stories in *The Barefoot Book of Tropical Tales*: Mr. Sampath Sembapperuma, Mr. Malinda Kumarasinha, Mr. Chinthaka Muthumala, Ms. Dammapali Visumperuma and Mr. Asthika Potuhera; Mr. Joseph Eliné Jacques, Mr. Robert Jacques, Mrs. Marlene Jacques and Professor Leslie Desmangles; Mrs. Catena Caban-Owen, Mrs. Linda Garcia and her sister Suico, Mrs. Dorcas Valasquez, Mrs. Judith De La Torre, Ms. Haydee Ayala and Miss Yolanda Negron; Mrs. Normah Khairudhin, Miss Siti Khairudhin and Miss Azlin Ramdan; Mr. Len Cabral, Dr. Althea Prince, Mr. Kama Kamanda and Mrs. Martine Hounsou.

I know full well that, however careful I may be, and no matter how eloquent, my retelling can never match that of the native storytellers of whose cultural heritage and oral traditions the stories in *The Barefoot Book of Tropical Tales* are a part. Therefore I apologize to those whose stories I have retold here for such flaws and failings as may be found in my adaptations. May they find in them something worthy of the timeless beauty and enduring power of their various folk tale traditions.

— RAOUF MAMA

BAREFOOT BOOKS publishes high-quality picture books for children of
all ages and specializes in the work of artists and writers from many cultures.
If you have enjoyed this book and would like to receive a copy
of our current catalog, please contact our New York office —
Barefoot Books Inc., 37 West 17th Street, 4th Floor East,
New York, New York, 10011
e-mail: ussales@barefoot-books.com
website: www.barefoot-books.com